You see, when the squirrel was even tinier, he had fallen out of his mommy's nest where he was then discovered and rescued by two very nice people—Jake and Betsy Beasley. It was the Beasleys who brought him to meet his new human mommy, Miss Lulabell.

Lulabell had cared for baby squirrels before and knew that puppy milk was exactly what this squirrel needed. It was she who gave him the name "Beasley." Beasley was so grateful he had been rescued by Miss Lulabell. He loved her and knew she would always keep him safe.

When he was about three-and-a-half weeks old and could not yet see, Beasley began to grow fur. No longer a naked, pink squirrel, he sported a big, bushy tail that was almost as long as his body! *What in the world am I going to do with this long tail?* Beasley thought.

This is my big, bushy tail! It is soft and *fluffy!*

I can balance using my tail

I can use it as a blanket

By week four, he could see Miss Lulabell and, of course, still
recognize her sweet voice and gentle touch. He was beyond thrilled.

Beasley became braver and stronger, and began crawling around
his cage. Eventually, he could crawl all around the cage with vim and
vigor. He loved his little cage, but he really wanted more adventure.

One day, he noticed a window and some brown and green things outside. *How wonderful! What are those?* he thought. Miss Lulabell saw he was looking at the window.

"Beasley," she said, "that is THE WILD! That's where you come from."

Beasley could not believe his little squirrel ears. *Surely, I did not come from THE WILD,* he thought.

It was almost as if Miss Lulabell could hear Beasley's thoughts because she said, "Yes, Beasley, you *did* come from THE WILD." She explained that THE WILD could be a dangerous place for young squirrels like Beasley.

Beasley was terrified. He thought, *I don't want to go into THE WILD. It doesn't look cozy and warm like my little cage. And who will take care of me?*

Miss Lulabell looked lovingly into Beasley's eyes and said, "Don't you worry about that now, my scruffy friend. You will know when the time is right for you to go back to THE WILD. Your Miss Lulabell will *always* be here for you, Beasley."

That night, Beasley had a terrible dream about THE WILD! He dreamed it was cold and dark. There were scary noises and it wasn't cozy at all. When he woke up, he decided right then and there: he would *never* go into THE WILD!

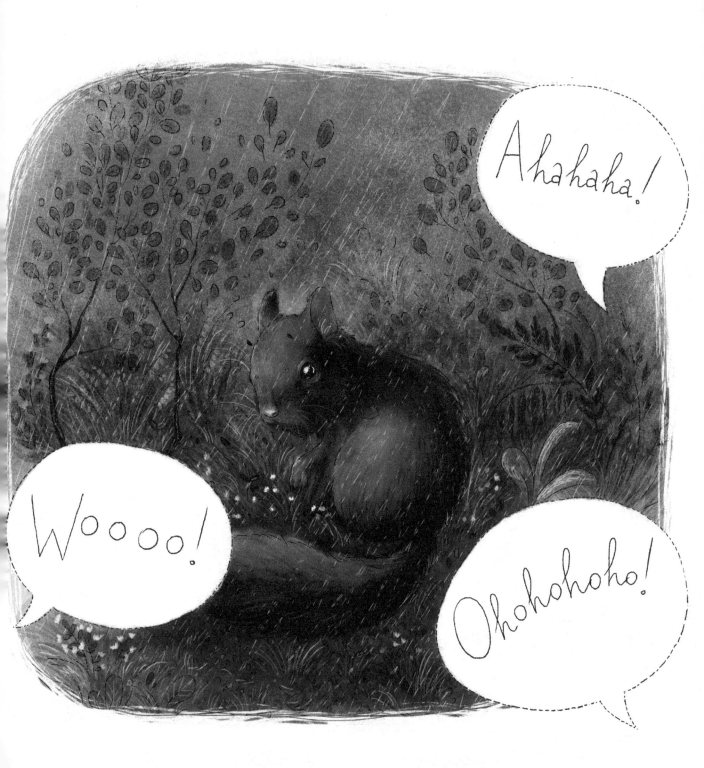

One crisp, October morning, when he was about two months old, Beasley had just finished a hearty breakfast of acorns, apples, and sweet potatoes. He peered out the window and noticed a beautiful, miniature house on the porch. *What is that?* he thought. *Could it be ... ?*

Miss Lulabell saw that Beasley was curious and said,
"Oh, I see you have noticed your new house. Would you
like to go take a look?"

*A new house! For me?* Beasley thought. *How exciting!*

Beasley was nervous. His new house looked charming and very enticing, but it was in THE WILD! He reluctantly crawled onto Miss Lulabell's arm, and she carried him out to the porch. Beasley couldn't remember being outside before.

Miss Lulabell opened the house's tiny door and said, "I made this for you, Beasley. You can come out to THE WILD anytime you want, and you will be protected in your little house."

Once he was inside, Beasley felt bright-eyed and bushy-tailed; he had a brand new place to play! In no time at all, he was scampering all over.

As the weeks went by, Beasley became braver and braver and less scared of THE WILD. And any time he peeked his fuzzy head outside, he would see other new friends who looked just like him.

He wanted to know them—and play with them too.

One afternoon, after a snack of grapes, Beasley
ventured out of his little house and into THE WILD.
He noticed it was not as bad as he thought. Plus, now
that he was almost six months old, he was stronger and
felt confident he would be safe.

He soon met two other squirrels named Charlie and
Sebastian. The three became friends almost immediately.
Charlie and Sebastian showed Beasley all their favorite
places to go in THE WILD.

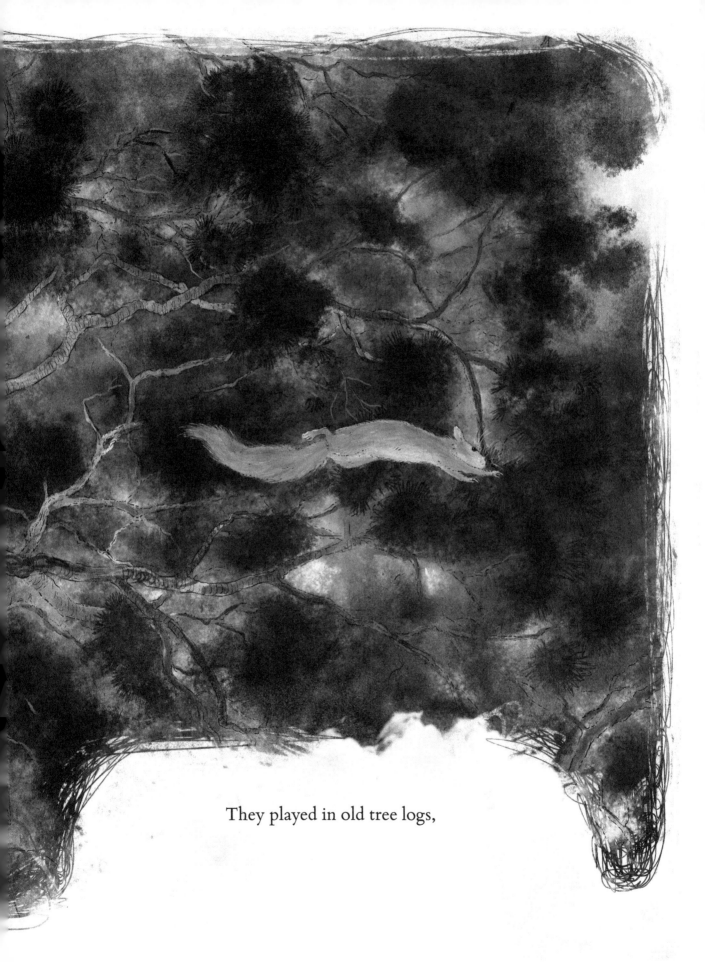

They played in old tree logs,

splashed in a creek,

and munched on wild blackberries.

Little by little, Beasley discovered that he loved THE WILD.
The place he had been so afraid of was not that scary after all—
especially with friends to keep him company.

Then on a drizzly, March morning, Beasley took Charlie and
Sebastian to his little house on Miss Lulabell's porch. At first,
Charlie and Sebastian were scared; their family had told them that
porches were in THE TAME PLACE. They did not want to go
there. In THE TAME PLACE were strange buildings and peculiar
animals who weren't very much fun. Plus, you weren't allowed to
chatter, scurry, or climb—or so they'd been told.

Beasley was shocked! All he could think about was how Miss Lulabell had been so kind and how she'd taken care of him when he was so tiny and could not see. When he explained this to his new friends, *they* were shocked. They had no idea THE TAME PLACE was an okay place to be.

Just then, Miss Lulabell came out with an
afternoon snack for Beasley. She immediately
noticed his new friends. She rushed into the house
to get more snacks so each of them would have
something to eat.

Charlie and Sebastian were amazed. They had never met a person before. Where was her tail? Where was her fur? Why did she smell like grapes? And why was she walking on two feet? Shouldn't she have four of them? Still, they loved the snacks Miss Lulabell brought out for them, and they came to learn that THE TAME PLACE was actually a good place. Beasley told them they could visit anytime.

As Beasley snuggled down in his slipper bed that night, he thought, *I was so scared of THE WILD, and then I met Charlie and Sebastian. They were scared of THE TAME PLACE, and then they met me. Maybe different is not so bad. Maybe different is just different.*

And with that, Beasley closed his eyes and drifted off to sleep.

CPSIA information can be obtained
at www.ICGtesting.com
Printed in the USA
BVHW020753220322
632081BV00005B/265